Speedy
SAM

**Other books in the
Shooting Star series:**

Abra Kadabra
 by Maureen Bayless

Howard's House is Haunted
 by Maureen Bayless

Mystery of the Lunchbox Criminal
 by Alison Lohans

Germy Johnson's Secret Plan
 by Alison Lohans

Project Disaster
 by Sylvia McNicoll

Princesses Don't Wear Jeans
 by Brenda Bellingham

Dragons Don't Read Books
 by Brenda Bellingham

Monsters in the School
 by Martyn Godfrey

Adventure in Legoland
 by Carol Matas

Safari Adventure in Legoland
 by Carol Matas

Speedy SAM

Dorothy Joan Harris

Illustrations by Kimberly Hart

Scholastic Canada Limited

Canadian Cataloguing in Publication Data

Harris, Dorothy Joan, 1931-
    Speedy Sam

(Shooting Star)
ISBN 0-590-73214-5
Issued also in French under title: Cléo, la souris express.

I. Hart, Kimberly. II. Title. III. Series.

PS8565.A6483S7   jC813'.54   C89-094449-0
PZ7.H37Sp 1991

6 5 4   Printed in Canada   3 4 5 6 7/9
                  Manufactured by Webcom Limited

For Irene and Hugh

Contents

Chapter 1

Early morning

It was Adam who saw the mouse first.

Adam Clark was up early that morning. He liked getting up early all by himself. In the Clarks' small apartment he didn't have many other chances to be alone.

Adam put the cereal box and the milk jug on the kitchen table and sat down on his favourite chair, the one beside the window. It had a little hole in its padded seat and some of the stuffing was coming out, but Adam still liked it best. And first thing in the morning when he got up early was practically the only time he got to sit in it.

Adam made himself comfortable, then spooned up some cornflakes and started reading the back of the cereal box. Cereal boxes were much more interesting than school readers. This one had a coupon on the back. If you sent off $5.95 plus the coupon you could get a plastic spacemobile. Adam didn't have $5.95, but he read the whole ad anyway.

The apartment was very quiet this early in the morning. Suddenly he heard a noise. Not a big noise, but something, over by the stove.

He left his breakfast and crept closer. There it was again, a little scratching noise.

He peeked carefully behind the stove. And there, looking straight up at him, was a small brown mouse. Its eyes were black and shiny and it didn't seem at all afraid.

"Hi, Mouse," whispered Adam. "Where did you come from?"

The mouse didn't answer.

"Want a cornflake?"

Adam fished a few cornflakes out of his bowl and dropped them on the floor beside the stove.

The mouse came out and sniffed at them, but not very eagerly.

"Don't you like cornflakes?" Adam asked.

He thought for a moment, then reached into the cookie jar. He wasn't supposed to eat cookies without asking his mom first, but he wasn't going to eat this one. He chose an oatmeal one and dropped a few bits on the floor.

The mouse sniffed the cookie crumbs. This time it began to eat right away.

"You like cookies, do you? Me too," Adam said.

He watched the mouse nibbling at the cookie crumbs, his own breakfast quite forgotten. Watching a mouse was much more fun than eating boring old cornflakes.

Before long Adam heard new noises. This time they were coming from the bedroom. His mom and his little sister Sarah must be getting up.

He heard his mom turn on the taps in the bathroom. A few minutes later Sarah danced into the kitchen.

"Why are you standing by the stove?" she asked.

Sarah's voice was not very big, so the mouse wasn't scared. It kept right on eating.

"Sh-h-h," said Adam all the same.

Sarah shushed and came closer.

"Oh," she squealed, "a cute little mousie!"

"Sh-h-h," warned Adam again. "Don't tell Mom. Promise?"

Sarah nodded. "I promise."

They both watched while the mouse ate up all the crumbs and began to clean its whiskers with its tiny paws. This was a very tidy mouse.

Then Adam heard his mom coming towards the kitchen. He hurried back to the table and his soggy cornflakes, dragging Sarah with him.

Their mother came in and went over to make herself some coffee. But as she reached for the kettle she glanced down at the floor and frowned.

"I can see some more stuffing from that padded chair on the floor," she said. "You children have been poking at the hole again."

"Not me," said Adam.

"Not me," said Sarah.

"Well, somebody has," their mother insisted.

"Maybe the mousie," said Sarah.

"Sarah!" Adam hissed. "You promised!"

Sarah clapped her hands over her mouth. But it was too late.

"Mousie?" said their mother. "What mouse?"

Neither Sarah nor Adam answered. But

Sarah couldn't help glancing over at the stove. Their mother noticed and went over to have a look for herself.

"Ee-eek!" she screamed. "A mouse!"

Adam jumped up from the table and ran to the stove. But the mouse had disappeared.

"You scared it," he told his mother. "It's gone into its hole."

"I scared it?" she answered. "It scared me! We'll have to catch it."

"Catch it?" said Sarah. "Can we keep it?"

"No. I've told you before we're not having any pets," said their mother. Then she stopped and frowned again, looking down at her watch. "Oh dear, I'm going to be late for work," she worried. "Hurry up and eat your breakfast, you two."

Adam poured some cereal and milk for Sarah. Their mother drank her coffee and made lunches for Adam and herself. Sarah stayed with a babysitter in their apartment building, so she didn't need a lunch.

As they hurried out the door a little later, Adam was still thinking about the mouse. His mom hadn't said anything more about it, he realized.

He hoped she'd forgotten it completely.

Chapter 2

The mousetrap

At school Adam's mind kept wandering to the mouse.

That sure is a cute mouse we have, he thought. I think I'll call him Sam.

He started a picture of Sam on his arithmetic paper. He drew big ears and long whiskers and shiny black eyes. Then he turned the paper over and drew a tail on the back. He spent so much time drawing that he didn't do much arithmetic.

His teacher, Mrs. Bain, noticed. She always noticed things like that. Some of the kids in the class had named her Bain the Pain.

"Adam!" she rumbled. "You only finished three questions."

Adam said nothing.

"What have you been doing all this time?" she demanded.

Adam still said nothing.

Mrs. Bain picked up his paper to have a closer look. She saw the tail he'd drawn by question 11. "What's this?" she asked.

"It's a tail," Adam explained. "A tail for the mouse I drew." He turned the paper over to show her.

Mrs. Bain studied the mouse for a moment. "That's a good drawing," she said at last. "Do you have a pet mouse?"

"Well . . . sort of."

"What's his name?"

"Sam."

"That's a good name," said Mrs. Bain. "But do you think you could turn your attention to this arithmetic if I gave you a few more minutes?"

Adam glanced quickly at the questions. "I think so."

"Okay then, get to work!"

Adam worked hard. He had to write a few of the answers on top of the mouse drawing. But it was still a good drawing, he thought.

At recess Jeremy and Phil came up to Adam.

"Do you really have a mouse?" Jeremy asked. "I thought your mom told you no pets."

"She did," said Adam.

"So how can you have a pet mouse?" asked Phil.

"I don't yet," Adam told him. "But I'm going to have one soon."

After school Adam went to the apartment where Sarah spent the day. The babysitter's name was Mrs. Velasquez. But that was too

hard to say in a hurry, so she let them call her Mrs. Vee.

Adam wondered whether Mrs. Vee had any mouseholes behind her stove. He took a quick peek and couldn't see any. He was glad because Mrs. Vee had a big orange cat called Fluffy.

Adam liked Fluffy. She often curled up on his lap when he was watching television. But he didn't want his mouse to come into Fluffy's apartment.

Adam's mother picked them up at six o'clock the way she always did. When they got to their own apartment, she took a small brown paper bag out of her purse.

"What's that?" asked Adam.

"A mousetrap."

So his mother hadn't forgotten. But maybe she had decided to help him catch the mouse to play with. "Can I see it? How does it work?" he asked.

"I'll show you later. First I've got to get supper started."

"Can we have macaroni and cheese for supper tonight?" Sarah said hopefully.

"Yes, I suppose so."

"Goody!" cheered Adam and Sarah together. That was their favourite meal.

"You two set the table while I get the water boiling for the macaroni," their mother went on.

Adam quickly set the table, not even trying to get Sarah to help him. By the time the macaroni was in the pot, he was finished.

"Can I see the trap now, Mom?" he begged.

She lifted the mousetrap out of the paper bag and set it on the floor.

"Be careful," she warned. "Don't come too close."

Adam watched from a distance.

"You pull this wire over and hook it under this spring," she explained. "Then when the mouse touches the spring—bang! It's caught."

Adam was horrified.

"But Mom!" he cried. "We can't use that! That would hurt our mouse. It would squash him!"

"Well, yes," said his mother. "But we do have to get rid of it."

"No — no —" Adam stammered.. "I wanted to catch it so I could have it as a pet."

"A pet?" His mother's face looked blank. "You know I said we couldn't have any pets, Adam. And you certainly can't keep that mouse for a pet."

"But Mom! You can't hurt him either. He's such a cute little thing, with pink ears and whiskers — you just can't!"

A tear rolled down Adam's cheek. Even his mother began to look rather upset. She put the mousetrap back in the paper bag.

"Never mind," she said. "We'll talk about this later. Supper's almost ready now. Go get Sarah, please."

Chapter 3

Speedy mouse

Adam didn't enjoy his favourite supper as much as he usually did. He was too busy worrying about that trap.

He was glad his mom had put it back in the bag. He figured maybe that was a sign she really didn't like it much either. After supper, when he'd dried the dishes, he sat down to think hard.

He was trying to remember a picture he'd

seen in a book somewhere. A picture of another trap, one that could catch animals without hurting them.

He could see it in his mind. The trap was a box propped up on a stick, he remembered, with some bait on the ground underneath. The stick had a string tied to it, and while the animal was eating the bait you just pulled the string. Then the box would fall and catch the animal inside.

If only he could build a trap like that and catch the mouse. Then his mom wouldn't have to set the other one.

Adam was sure it would work, but first he needed a box. A shoebox would be just the right size. And only last week Sarah had gotten a new pair of running shoes with little rabbits on them.

Sarah was in her bedroom. "Can I borrow your rabbit shoebox for a while?" he asked her.

"What for?"

"To help me catch the mouse."

Sarah stuck out her lower lip. "That box is my doll's bed now."

"You can have it back as soon as the mouse is caught," Adam promised. "I won't hurt your box. Honest."

"Will you hurt the mouse?"

"No. At least I hope not," he added. "But the trap Mom bought will squash him flat. You don't want him squashed flat, do you?"

Sarah shook her head firmly. But she still looked doubtful.

"How can my shoebox catch a mouse?" she asked.

"Let me have it and I'll show you."

Sarah reached under the bed and slowly pulled out her shoebox. It had little dancing rabbits all along the sides of the box. She lifted out her rag doll and the remains of her baby blanket.

"Here," she said, holding out the box.

"Thanks," he said as he took it.

Adam carried the shoebox into the kitchen. Sarah followed him. He got a ruler from the drawer and tied a piece of string to it. Then he propped up one end of the box with the ruler and laid the string carefully along the floor.

Their mother found them sitting on the floor.

"What are you two doing?" she asked.

"We're going to catch the mousie," Sarah said excitedly. "And we're using my rabbit shoebox."

"Oh," she said. "I see."

Adam saw her look strangely at him, but she didn't sound cross. He figured that was another good sign.

"Please, Mom," he pleaded. "Please let me try to catch the mouse this way."

"Well . . ."

Adam held his breath.

"Okay," she said at last. "I guess you can try it. What are you going to use as bait?"

"Cookies," Adam told her.

"Cookies?" she said. "Are you sure mice like cookies?"

"This one does."

There was only one oatmeal cookie left. Adam crumbled it and piled the crumbs under the propped-up box.

Sarah wanted to eat some of the bigger chunks, so Adam fished a few out and gave them to her. After all, it was her shoebox.

The two of them sat down on the floor by the end of the string and waited. But nothing happened. No mouse appeared. Sarah got bored and went off to watch television instead. Then it was her bedtime and Adam could hear his mother reading her a story. But he still sat where he was, waiting.

When Sarah was settled down to sleep his mother came back into the kitchen. "Are you going to sit there all evening, Adam?" she asked.

He nodded.

"You're missing your favourite program," she told him.

"I know."

His mother looked at him for a moment.

Then she came and sat down on the floor beside him. "I'll help you watch," she said.

It was nice sitting there with his mom. They talked a little, in whispers, and Adam told her about the mouse drawing on his arithmetic paper.

Then, at last, they heard a soft scratching noise. And soon they saw the mouse scamper out from behind the stove.

They both sat very still. The mouse didn't notice them at all. He darted this way and that. Soon he had found the pile of cookie crumbs.

At first he just nibbled on the crumbs around the edge of the pile. Adam waited. He wanted the mouse right under the box.

It seemed like forever before the mouse finally moved in close enough to the crumbs, but as soon as he did, Adam pulled the string!

He had been quick.

But the mouse was even quicker. Before the ruler and box could fall, he was gone.

He raced back behind the stove and disappeared.

Adam and his mother just looked at each other.

"That's a real speedy mouse," Adam said admiringly.

"Yes," his mother agreed.

"Pretty clever too."

"Yes," she said again. Then she frowned. "But, Adam, we do have to catch it, even if it is clever."

"Not with that wire mousetrap!" Adam cried. "Let me try one other way first."

His mother hesitated.

"Please!" begged Adam.

"Well . . . okay. One more try. But how are you going to do it?"

Chapter 4

No luck

Adam was busy asking himself that same question. How else could he try to catch the mouse without hurting him?

He sat down and thought hard. He thought about all the animal programs he'd seen on television. Some had been about catching wild beasts. Could he remember anything from them that might help? Suddenly his face brightened.

"I know!" he said. "We could make a tiger trap. I saw one on a nature program once. The hunters dug a hole in the ground and put branches over it, and then the tiger fell through and —"

But his mother was shaking her head. "Adam! We can't dig a hole in the kitchen floor."

"No-o-o," Adam agreed.

They both sat in silence for a moment.

"I wonder . . ." his mother spoke slowly. "I wonder if it would work with an above-ground hole."

"A what?"

"An above-ground hole. We could use something like the big metal wastebasket in your room."

Adam's eyes widened with excitement. "Hey, that's a good idea! We could put a plank up to the top of the wastebasket and put cookies inside it. Then when the mouse jumped in after the cookies, it would be caught!"

"Yes," his mother agreed. "I don't think the mouse would be able to climb up the inside of the wastebasket. But what would you use as a plank?"

That was a puzzler. It would have to be quite long, and sturdy too. Adam thought for a while.

"I guess," he said at last, "I could use that dinosaur poster I drew last year. It's made of strong cardboard. I could cut a strip off of it to use for a plank."

"Oh, Adam, are you sure you want to use that?"

Adam wasn't at all sure that he wanted to cut up his dinosaur poster. He'd gotten a gold star for it. But he couldn't think of anything else in the apartment that would do.

"I'm sure," he said. Then he added, "Maybe I can stick it back together afterwards."

Adam brought the wastebasket and his poster to the kitchen. He cut a long narrow strip off the side of the poster and fastened one end to the top of the wastebasket.

"The oatmeal cookies are all gone," he told his mother, "so I'll have to use a chocolate chip one instead. But I'm sure the mouse will like that too."

It was late by the time everything was ready. Adam went off to bed, but he knew he wasn't going to sleep. He was going to stay awake and listen. As soon as he heard any little mouse noises he would get up and creep back to the kitchen and . . .

But he didn't stay awake. He didn't even wake up early in the morning. The next noise he heard was his mother calling, "Come on, Adam, time to get ready for school."

Adam jumped up and ran to the kitchen. The trap was still there, but so were the cookie crumbs. And there was no mouse to be seen.

"I guess it didn't work," he said sadly to his mother.

"No. It didn't."

"Maybe the mouse was just too scared to come back again last night," he suggested. "Maybe it'll come tonight."

He looked hopefully at his mom while he said this. But she was looking over at the counter where the bag with the wire mousetrap still sat.

"We have to catch that mouse, Adam," was all she said.

Chapter 5

Mrs. Bain helps

Adam walked to school feeling very gloomy. He knew he couldn't stall his mom much longer. In his mind he could see that wire trap and the way it would go *sproing*. Poor little mouse . . .

He was still thinking about it when recess came. Instead of running outside with the rest of the class when the bell rang, he stayed back and went to the teacher's desk.

"Um-m, Mrs. Bain," he began, "are you afraid of mice?"

Mrs. Bain looked only a little surprised. "No," she answered. "Why?"

Adam stared at the floor and scuffed his shoes. Maybe this was a mistake, he thought, asking Bain the Pain for advice. He scuffed his shoes some more.

Finally Mrs. Bain spoke up. "Is this about your pet mouse?" she asked.

"Well, it's not exactly a pet," said Adam. "Not yet. It comes out from behind our stove at night. But my mom says we have to catch it. She bought a mousetrap. Do you know what mousetraps do?"

Mrs. Bain nodded.

"They go *sproing* on the poor mouse," Adam told her, just to make sure she understood. "That's horrible. So I wanted to catch the mouse first. I remembered seeing a picture of a box propped up on a stick with —"

"That's a picture in our reader," Mrs. Bain put in.

Adam stopped in amazement. "In our reader?" he said. He could hardly believe it. Readers didn't usually have anything good in them.

"Yes, that was in one of the first stories we read this year," Mrs. Bain told him. "Didn't it work for you?"

"No. It wasn't fast enough. This is a really speedy mouse," Adam said admiringly.

"Most mice are pretty speedy," Mrs. Bain agreed. She sounded admiring too. She didn't sound like a pain at all.

Adam went on.

"So then I tried another kind of trap. I set up my big wastebasket with a plank leading to the edge so the mouse could climb up and jump inside. Only that didn't work either."

"Oh?" Mrs. Bain looked thoughtful. "What did you put in the wastebasket for bait?"

"Cookies. This mouse likes cookies."

"Mmm, maybe so. But I think you need something with a good strong smell to tempt it into the basket. Why don't you try putting peanut butter in there?"

"Peanut butter? Do mice like peanut butter?"

"They sure do. And you should put some dabs of it on the plank too. Just little dabs, mind you — you don't want the mouse to get full up before you've coaxed him into your trap."

"Right," said Adam, nodding wisely.

"You'll let me know how it works, won't you?"

"Sure," he promised. He looked down and scuffed his shoes again. "Uh, thanks, Mrs. Bain," he blurted suddenly. Then he ran out of the room for recess.

Just outside the classroom door Adam found Jeremy waiting for him.

"So that's how you're getting your pet mouse," Jeremy began.

"No fair!" said Adam. "You were listening!"

"Hey, don't get mad," said Jeremy. "I

think it's a neat idea."

"You do?"

"Sure. What are you going to call him?"

"I've already named him," Adam answered. "He's Sam. Speedy Sam."

"And where are you going to keep him after you've caught him?"

Adam heaved a sigh. "That's another problem," he admitted.

"Well," said Jeremy, "there's a pet shop over on Elm Street. Let's go after school and see if they have any mouse cages."

After school the two boys hurried over to Elm Street. The pet shop had plenty of mouse cages just right for a little brown mouse. But they all cost a lot of money.

"Twenty-four dollars just for a cage?" Adam whispered as they studied the price tags. "With nothing inside it?"

"A real rip-off," Jeremy agreed.

He didn't even ask if Adam had twenty-four dollars. He knew he didn't. "Maybe you could get one for your birthday," he

suggested. "Roger got a ten-speed bike for his birthday today. A red one."

"He did?" Adam was impressed. Nobody else in the third grade had a ten-speed. "But my birthday's not for months yet."

"Too bad," said Jeremy.

The boys left the pet shop and Adam walked slowly home. It was late when he finally reached Mrs. Vee's apartment.

"I was starting to get worried," said Mrs. Vee.

"Jeremy and I went to the pet shop to look at mouse cages," Adam explained.

Mrs. Vee raised her eyebrows in surprise. "Do you have a mouse?"

"Sort of. There's a little brown one that comes out from behind our stove at night."

"Oh, that sort of mouse. I'll lend you Fluffy for a few days if you want. She'll soon get rid of it for you."

Adam looked over at the chair where Fluffy was sleeping. She stirred and gave a yawn. Adam could see her pink tongue and lots of sharp white teeth.

"No!" he cried. He could almost feel those sharp white teeth. "No! I don't want to get rid of the mouse. I want to keep him."

"You do?" said Mrs. Vee. "Does your mother know that?"

"Not yet," said Adam sadly.

Chapter 6

Success!

Whe Adam and his mother and Sarah went into their apartment that night, the wastebasket was still by the stove.

"Put that basket back in your room, Adam," ordered his mother. "We'll trip over it in here."

Adam's heart sank. Maybe she wasn't going to let him try the trap again. He put the basket back in his room, but as soon as supper was over he brought it out again.

"I told my teacher about the trap," he said to his mom. "She thinks we should try using peanut butter as bait."

"Peanut butter?"

"Yes," Adam said firmly. "She said the trap is sure to work then."

That wasn't exactly what Mrs. Bain had said, but he had to convince his mom somehow. Adam set to work quickly with the peanut butter, putting dabs of it inside the basket and on the plank.

To his relief his mom didn't stop him. She really didn't seem very eager to use the wire trap either. All she said was, "That peanut butter will stain your poster, you know."

"I know," Adam said.

His mother watched him arrange the trap again.

"Perhaps we should smear a little oil on the inside of the basket," she suggested. "Just to make sure the sides are too slippery for the mouse to climb back out."

"That's a good idea," Adam agreed happily.

After the trap was set Adam went off to bed. That night he tried even harder to stay awake, but again he fell asleep. The next morning he woke up really early. He jumped out of bed and ran to the kitchen.

"Mom!" he shouted. "Our trap worked! We caught the mouse. Come and see!"

His mother came hurrying into the kitchen. So did Sarah.

"Oh, what a cute mousie!" Sarah cooed.

"Is he hurt?" Adam asked worriedly. "He's not moving around much."

His mother watched for a moment. "No. I think he's just too full to run around — full of our peanut butter!"

The peanut butter was certainly gone, every bit. And the mouse had a rather sleepy look on his face.

"We've invented a new kind of mousetrap," Adam said proudly.

"Yes," agreed his mother. "But now that

we've caught the mouse, what do we do with it?"

"We could keep him," Adam suggested slowly, "right in the wastebasket."

But even as he spoke he knew that wasn't a very good idea. The wastebasket was nothing like the cages in the pet shop. And his mom was shaking her head sternly.

"No way," she said. "No."

Adam knew she meant what she said. He sat down on the floor beside the trap and tried to think of a solution.

"Maybe I could take the mouse to school with me," he suggested. "I could put it in with the hamster in the kindergarten class." He looked over at his mom. She wasn't shaking her head, so he went on.

"Could I borrow your box to take the mouse to school, Sarah?" he asked.

"My shoebox? My rabbit shoebox?" Sarah said with a worried frown.

"I won't hurt it," Adam promised.

"The mouse might."

"How could a little mouse hurt your box? Especially a sleepy little mouse like Sam?"

"Is that his name?" she asked.

"Yes. Do you like Sam for a name?"

Sarah hesitated. Adam knew he'd won.

"Okay," she said. "You can use my shoebox for Sleepy Sam."

Adam transferred the mouse gently into Sarah's rabbit shoebox. His mother tied the box tightly with string.

Adam was too excited to eat much breakfast, so he hurried off to school long before the other two were ready. And since he was so early he decided to go past the pet shop.

The shop was still closed. But inside, Adam could see the storekeeper talking to some of the animals.

Adam knocked on the glass window and pointed to his box. The storekeeper came to the door with a puzzled look on his face.

"Do you buy pet mice?" Adam asked him quickly.

"Sometimes," said the storekeeper.

"What colour are your mice?"

"I've only got one," Adam said. "He's brown. Do you want to see him?"

The storekeeper shook his head. "I only have white mice."

"But brown is just as nice as white! And this one is really cute."

"No," said the storekeeper, shaking his head again. "Sorry."

There was nothing else for Adam to do. He tucked the shoebox carefully under his arm and went on to school. When he reached the schoolyard he could see a crowd of boys over by the bicycle racks.

"What's up?" he asked, joining the crowd.

"Roger brought his new bike to school," Jeremy answered.

"Wow!" said Adam.

He put the shoebox down on the ground and wriggled his way through the crowd. "Can I sit on it, Roger?" he asked. "Can I?"

"Sure," Roger agreed. He was pleased with all the attention his bike was getting.

"You'll have to wait your turn though," Jason put in. "I'm next."

Everyone wanted a turn sitting on Roger's bike. He let them each have one minute, as long as they didn't touch the gears. They were still crowded around the racks when the nine o'clock bell rang.

Adam quickly scooped up the shoebox from the ground and tucked it back under his arm. He ran to line up with all the other boys, then hurried ahead to his classroom.

"Mrs. Bain," he cried, "the peanut butter worked! Just the way you said it would. I brought the mouse with me and —"

Suddenly he stopped and stared at the box in his hand. A ragged hole had appeared in one corner. And when Adam peered in, there was no little brown mouse to be seen.

Chapter 7

Mouse at large

Oh, no!" cried Adam. "I've lost my mouse! He's gone!"

He stared at the box in dismay. "And he's wrecked Sarah's box too. There's a hole right through one of the dancing rabbits."

Mrs. Bain took the box from Adam. She untied the string and lifted the lid.

"Your mouse is definitely gone," she

agreed. "Were you bringing it to show the class?"

"Not exactly," Adam told her. "My mom said I couldn't keep him at home. So I thought maybe I could put him in with the hamster in the kindergarten room. There's lots of room in that cage."

"Oh, Adam." Mrs. Bain was shaking her head. "That wouldn't have worked. The hamster would probably attack a little mouse."

"It would?"

"Yes. Maybe even eat it."

Adam gulped at the thought. Nobody seemed to like his mouse.

Nobody except Mrs. Bain. "Where was the box when your mouse got out?" she asked. "On the playground?"

Adam nodded.

"Well then," said Mrs. Bain, "he's probably found a little hole for himself by now. And you know, Adam, he'll be much happier out there than in a cage."

"But what will he find to eat out there?" Adam asked worriedly.

"I dropped part of a doughnut on the playground yesterday," one of the girls in the class spoke up. "He can have that."

"And I've got some peanuts in my lunch," Jeremy put in. "I'll leave some of them outside for Sam."

"Is that still what you call him? Sam?" said Mrs. Bain.

"Speedy Sam," Adam nodded. He was starting to feel much better.

Then he remembered Sarah's box. "But what about the hole in the box? I promised my sister the mouse wouldn't hurt her rabbit box."

"Let me have a look." Mrs. Bain studied it for a moment. "Hmm. I have some green tape in my desk. We could put some strips of it all around the box as decoration. We could even make them look like grass for the rabbits to dance on. And then we could put some extra pieces where the hole is."

Mrs. Bain took the sticky tape out of her desk. While the class did arithmetic she put green strips, like grass, all around the box.

Adam thought the box looked nicer than ever like that. And he decided he had a new, better name for Mrs. Bain. From now on she'd be Bain the Brain. He'd tell the rest of the kids at recess.

When Sarah saw the decoration on her shoebox after school she was delighted. She took the box and ran to show it to Mrs. Vee.

"My dolly can pretend to be sleeping out in the meadow now," she announced happily.

Adam didn't mention the hole at all. He just explained that his teacher thought the rabbits needed some grass to dance on.

When his mother got home she asked, "What did you do with the mouse, Adam?"

"I let him go," he told her.

"Good. That was probably the best idea." She put some water on for macaroni and cheese again. "Set the table, please."

Adam took knives and forks out of the drawer. But as he began to put them around the table he noticed something on the floor.

It was more stuffing from the seat of his favourite chair. And it hadn't been there that morning, he knew.

Adam said nothing to his mom. But he decided not to glue his poster back together just yet.

He figured he was going to have another Speedy Sam before long.